Madeleine Vinton Dahlgren

The social-official etiquette of the United States

Madeleine Vinton Dahlgren

The social-official etiquette of the United States

ISBN/EAN: 9783741194535

Manufactured in Europe, USA, Canada, Australia, Japa

Cover: Foto ©Andreas Hilbeck / pixelio.de

Manufactured and distributed by brebook publishing software
(www.brebook.com)

Madeleine Vinton Dahlgren

The social-official etiquette of the United States

The Social-Official Etiquette of the United States, by Madeleine Vinton Dahlgren.

SIXTH EDITION.

BALTIMORE:

JOHN MURPHY & COMPANY,

1894.

Preface.

WHEN the fifth edition of this little work on the "Etiquette of Social Life in Washington" was issued, it was desired anew to express gratification at the favorable reception it has met with, and also to renew my thanks for the assurances received from many official personages, as well as others of distinction in our society here, that the views herein given are considered correct and logical, *and are accepted as authority.*

I have been repeatedly requested to enlarge this treatise on the *peculiarities* of Washington Social Life, so as to combine with it a Manual of Etiquette, and make it a text-book of good breeding. While very sensible of the implied compliment of supposing that I am capable of giving such large instructions as would form polished manners, yet I would be appalled at the magnitude of such an undertaking!

There is a trite saying, "that it takes three generations to make a lady or a gentleman." Although I can in no wise admit a statement so greatly at variance with the most cherished maxims of our republican institutions, which justly base all distinc-

3

tion upon personal merit alone, yet this axiom of the Old World has this significance for us: It implies that sensibility is an innate gift which must be "born with us," and no book or set of rules ever written or invented can confer refinement where the nature is coarse and the education has been neglected. I, therefore, hold in slight estimation all treatises purporting to form good manners, which, to be genuine, must have a deeper foundation than any book can give. But the *official* life here leads to perplexing social questions, and demands a special code of social laws to meet it; and this is the peculiar phase of life at the seat of government that this "Etiquette" is intended to explain.

I have not, therefore, materially enlarged my first work, other than to add a chapter to the Appendix with regard to "Some Points" which had not at first been elucidated with the requisite care.

In presenting a sixth edition, I have tried to make such revision as is needed, in order to meet changes made by several laws recently enacted, which by their reflex action bear upon social-official usage.

It has been suggested that the rapidly increasing demands of Washington life require some change of hitherto accepted forms in order to make it possible to meet the weight of social obligation. These contemplated innovations I shall allude to.

The charming musical fragment, "*If order is Heaven's first law,*" was written by the great *maestro*

Hans von Bülow as a prelude to the fifth edition of "Etiquette of Social Life in Washington," and presented with the request to have it so published. I am happy to give it the first place, which it so well merits, and do so as a tribute of respect to this gifted artist.

"If Order is Heaven's First Law."

which may tend to a-void con - fu - sion in so - cial

life.

Because we are a Re-public,

we are not ne-ces-sa-ri-ly to be. deprived of

8

those a - me - ni - ties which ren-der life a-

mf *grazioso.*

p *dolce.*

greeable,

espr.

and as-

sist to cul - ti - vate, to cul - ti - vate good

mf

feel - - - ing.

espr.

which may tend to a-void con - fu - sion in so - cial

life.

Because we are a Re-public,

we are not ne-ces-sa-ri-ly to be deprived of

8

those a - me - ni - ties   which ren-der life a-

mf *grazioso.*   *p*   *dolce.*

greeable,   and as-

espr.

sist   to cul - ti-vate, to cul - ti-vate good

mf

feel - - - - ing.

f espr.

9

which may tend to a-void con-fu-sion in so-cial

life.

Because we are a Re-public,

Cour-te-sy may be con - sidered but as the mir-ror of

Cha - ri - ty; and, al-though it may

oft - en become an un - mean - ing semblance of be-

nevolence, yet, yet, yet if

10

we as-si-du-ous-ly cul-ti-vate, if on-ly but a

shadow, we may fi - nal-ly hope to gain . . . . the re-

al - i-ty.   Since e - - go-tism

is   the most   dreaded bane of so-ci - e-ty,

11

meno mosso.

if we can learn so far to forget our - selves as to con-

sid - er the just claims of oth - ers, the

just claims of oth - ers, we shall have

gained, we shall have gained a

12

great vic-to-ry, a vic-to-ry o - ver self - ish-

ness; for that which is called

good breed - ing is ac-tu-al-ly the

gold-en rule car-ried in - to prac-tice,

13

14

Social-Official Etiquette.

I F order is Heaven's first law, we should not regard as beneath careful attention the proper recognition of rules which may tend to avoid confusion in social life.

Because we are a republic we are not necessarily to be deprived of those amenities which render life agreeable and assist to cultivate good feeling.

Courtesy may be considered but as the mirror of charity, and, although it may often become an unmeaning semblance of benevolence, yet, if we assiduously cultivate, if only but the shadow, we may finally hope to gain the reality. Thus, by placing ourselves in excellent relations towards others, we may eventually acquire that sentiment of good will which may at first have been but a mere appearance.

That which is called good breeding is actually the Golden Rule carried into practice, and is therefore a very Christian accomplishment. Since egotism is the most dreaded bane of society, if we can learn so far to forget ourselves as to consider the just claims of others, we shall have gained a victory over selfishness. But my intention is not to moralize or

15

"If Order is Heaven's First Law."

which may tend to a - void con - fu - sion in so - cial

life.

Because we are a Re - public,

we are not ne - ces - sa - ri - ly to be deprived of

those a - me - ni - ties   which ren-der   life a-

greeable,   and as-

sist   to   cul - ti-vate,   to   cul - ti-vate good

feel . . . ing.

9

Cour-te-sy may be con-sidered but as the mir-ror of

Cha - ri - ty; and, al-though it may

oft - en become an un-mean-ing semblance of be-

nevolence, yet, yet, yet if

10

we as-si-du-ous-ly cul-ti-vato, if on-ly but a

shadow, we may 'fi - nal-ly hope to gain . . . . the re-

al - i-ty. Since e - - go-tism

is the most dreaded bane of so-ci - e-ty,

meno mosso.

if we can learn so far to forget our-selves as to con-

sid - er the just claims of oth - ers, the

Animato.

just claims of oth - ers, we shall have

gained, we shall have gained a

12

great vic-to-ry, a vic-to-ry o - ver self-ish-

ness; for that which is called

good breed - ing is ac-tu-al-ly the

gold-en rule car-ried in - to prac-tice,

13

and is therefore a 've-ry Christian,

a ve-ry Chris-tian, a Chris-tian ac-

com - plish - ment.

14

Social-Official Etiquette.

I F order is Heaven's first law, we should not regard as beneath careful attention the proper recognition of rules which may tend to avoid confusion in social life.

Because we are a republic we are not necessarily to be deprived of those amenities which render life agreeable and assist to cultivate good feeling.

Courtesy may be considered but as the mirror of charity, and, although it may often become an unmeaning semblance of benevolence, yet, if we assiduously cultivate, if only but the shadow, we may finally hope to gain the reality. Thus, by placing ourselves in excellent relations towards others, we may eventually acquire that sentiment of good will which may at first have been but a mere appearance.

That which is called good breeding is actually the Golden Rule carried into practice, and is therefore a very Christian accomplishment. Since egotism is the most dreaded bane of society, if we can learn so far to forget ourselves as to consider the just claims of others, we shall have gained a victory over selfishness. But my intention is not to moralize or

15

present trite truisms, but to place within the scope
of a few pages the true state of the present phase of
Washington society life.

There are several unsettled questions with regard
to which I do not, of course, expect or intend to
do more than to indicate how it seems to me that
these points may be amicably adjusted.

Washington society life is principally official, or,
rather, society here is composed in so great a degree
of official personages who represent the mechanism
of the state, that the social obligations and customs
have become about as complex as the constitutional
laws upon which the official are based, and yet we
have no constitution or defined code which makes
our social laws as clear as our political. Yet this
should be the case.

No reader of history, however superficial his view,
but must have noticed how constantly the gravest
affairs of state have become complicated with the
thousand seeming nothings of every-day life. Nor
have we in America been at all exempt from such
entanglements. On the contrary, every one at all
familiar with the past social incidents of Washington
is perfectly aware of various occasions in which ani-
mosities have been engendered by the omission, or
the commission, of certain requirements exacted by
some and not so understood by others. It is,
indeed, extraordinary that this subject has not compelled a more explicit understanding long ago, in

view of the many embarrassments, and some of them not unimportant, that have already arisen from alternate neglect or ignorance of social observances which, in order to avoid confusion, should be well understood and carefully weighed.

Nor can ignorance of the official etiquette prevailing here be construed into any want of general society training elsewhere, because we have in Washington a very exceptional basis.

When the republic was first organized, we all know that the venerated Washington and his stately wife compelled a rigid observance of social etiquette towards the administration in its various branches. Jefferson, in consequence of his radical sentiments, introduced various innovations, but General Jackson, when he became President, first broke down the barriers of careful respect, and received all comers without any formal or special rules; and the consequence was that a disorder and rudeness characterized those receptions hitherto unknown, and which no private gentleman in the country would have tolerated in his own home.

If our stanch republicanism renders us unwilling to acknowledge that the President and his wife are the "first gentleman and lady" of the land, yet we may assuredly, without danger to our social independence, accord them socially that respectful deference which the Constitution gives to the Executive in the exercise of his granted prerogatives. Beginning

2

here, one may well concede to the various Departments that social recognition which is in harmony with the Constitution.

Not a winter passes but the same questions are asked over and over again by scores of persons entering for the first time into public life, or by strangers who come here to participate in our social festivities, who do not know what are the peculiar social requirements the official element has introduced. I may justly commence my remarks upon these peculiar exigencies by a consideration of the position of the Presidential family.

The President, as the executive head of the nation, is properly entitled to precedence. This first place is, of course, accorded to him whenever and wherever he appears in social life. His social privileges entitle him to receive all calls without being expected to return any. In conversation he is addressed as "Mr. President." Some choose to use the phrase "Your Excellency," but this is a matter of taste only. Usage has not required any special preliminary formalities in order to make the acquaintance of the President. During the session of Congress he gives stated receptions, and all persons who desire to do so may attend these levees. Upon entrance you give your name to an usher and are announced. You are thereupon introduced to the President by the Marshal of the District, or, at times, by some other person who may have been designated for such purpose, and you are immediately after presented to the different members of the Presidential family who may be present. Occasionally some embarrassment has arisen because persons on entering, in place of merely giving their own name to the official who makes the presentations, stop to introduce the friends who accompany them. This causes a delay, which arrests the throng of persons who are coming in, and consequent confusion ensues. In making this suggestion I refer, of course, only to the *public levees*, which are usually much crowded, and where a positive form of introduction insures equal justice to all.

In case you are precise, you leave your card before your departure from the Executive Mansion. If the reception is held in the morning, the usual costume for morning receptions suffices. ' If in the evening, a full toilette is demanded. It is not respectful to appear in less than evening dress at an evening reception given by the President. Even in making an evening call, at any time, it is more proper to appear in full dress. Those ladies who are fastidious do not wear a bonnet in making an evening visit at the President's. I have seen the wives of Foreign Ministers call *en grande-toilette.* If the President have a wife, she also receives the first visit from every one, nor is she expected to return any visits. Of course, if she desires to be especially kind, she is at liberty to make visits, although we believe it has been found a safer rule not to make distinctions. But other members of the Presidential family are allowed by custom to return visits and acknowledge civilities tendered. At the state dinners of the President the usual etiquette prevails as at other dinner-tables where official personages are entertained.

It is not permissible to decline a dinner or other invitation of a social nature sent by the President, unless in case of your own illness or that of any member of your family, or of the death of a relative. When, however, it is imperative to send a regret, explain in your note the reasons which compel a non-acceptance. Indeed, it is more respectful to state the cause rather than to send a merely formal regret, whenever an excuse of sufficient gravity may be assigned; so that it may plainly be understood that your absence is unavoidable.

This may also apply to other invitations which you desire to treat with especial consideration. Any invitation of a social nature extended by the President of the United States must be considered, by courtesy, as a command; and, therefore, it is allowable to waive all other previous engagements made which may conflict with your acceptance, even if it happen to be a dinner. But in no other instance may an invitation to dine, once accepted, be revoked; and even in such case you should mention the nature of the obligation which compels you.

The United States is so vast a nation, and the requirements upon the time and attention of the President are so pressing and unceasing, that the physical possibility of meeting the demands of the exalted position becomes a serious matter. The arrangement of the Executive Mansion, assigned to the President for such various uses, would seem, greatly to add to the weight of the burden which has to be borne. This mansion, even in the present youth of this great country, is already hallowed by so many interesting associations that it has become dear to the hearts of the people, and it must ever be regarded as a place of treasured memories. But, in point of fact, the country, by reason of its immense and increasing development, now requires a more liberal provision to be made as to the surroundings of the President of the United States.

The present Executive Mansion does not exceed in size, if, indeed, it is sufficient, for *executive* and *official* purposes,—we mean for the transaction of public business and for all official acts. Belonging to *the purely official life* should be classed the public levees, the state dinners, and all formal presentations and receptions.

The present Executive Mansion should be held and assigned *exclusively* to these purposes; but there should also be erected *a home* for the President,— a spot more secure from intrusion,—where, after the official round of duties has been met, he may

claim and obtain for some slight portion of each
day a measure of that dignified retiracy which is the
privilege of every other gentleman of consideration
in the land. Then, to be presented privately to the
President and his family *in their home circle,* should,
as in the days of our beloved Washington, require
the same evidence of respectable social standing that
other gentlemen of refinement expect in the choice of
their special acquaintances and personal friends.

Whenever a *Presidential* Mansion, in addition to
the present Executive Mansion, shall be provided,
it will be found to solve many displeasing problems
that now exist, and to spare much harassing fatigue
now involved. As it is, the need for rest from routine and for change of air are alike so imperative,
that at one time it grew into a sort of custom that
the President should become the guest of the invalid
soldiers at their home during the summer. It is
quite disgraceful that the nation should fail to make
their elected chief magistrate their own honored guest
at all times; but surely all that may be needed, is.
to call attention to the insufficiency of the present
arrangements, and point out how very incommen-
surate they are with the dignity of the country.

Certainly no country exceeds our own in large
expenditure, where any measure is once recognized
as necessary; and here I crave permission to call
attention to that apartment known by courtesy as
"the State Dining-Room" of the present Executive

Mansion. This room is miserably small for a banquet-hall. Its size will not permit over forty guests to be comfortably seated at a dinner; and this number can never represent the various elements that should meet at a state dinner. The nation should provide a banqueting-hall of sufficient space to entertain, upon occasions of state, the Justices of the Supreme Court, the Cabinet, the Senate and the Diplomatic Corps at one dinner.

The President may properly be addressed in writing as "His Excellency, the President of the United States," or as "President of the United States." The various members of the Cabinet are to be addressed respectively, in writing, as "The Honorable, the Secretary of State," "The Honorable, the Secretary of the Treasury," "The Honorable, the Secretary of War," "The Honorable, the Attorney-General," "The Honorable, the Postmaster-General," "The Honorable, the Secretary of the Navy," and "The Honorable, the Secretary of the Interior," etc.; the Vice-President and the Chief Justice as Mr. Vice-President and Mr. Chief Justice. Do not abbreviate words in sending a ceremonious note. When an official title, as in the case of diplomatic functionaries, is very long, whatever portion of the prefix you give, use the entire word, and then add "etc., etc.," in an under line, which is supposed to include all that is claimed.

All abbreviations are in bad taste in formal notes, whatever may be the title, whether civic, military,

or naval. The word " Present," written on an en-
velope, formerly much used, is now quite obsolete,
except as confined to communications of a business
nature, such as bills sent, and the word *Addressed*
or the French words " *En Ville* " have superseded
its use. Although decidedly opposed to the introduction of Gallicisms, as likely to emasculate the
vigorous Saxon of our noble language, yet in matters
of polite usage one may well continue to imitate our
ancestors and introduce the courtly Norman phrases :
they so aptly turn aside the blunt edge of much that
is disagreeable in this busy, material life we lead.
But I do object to that hybrid term, the "*Republican Court*," which we so often hear. It is senseless,
and an anomaly ; or if it have a meaning, it is still
more to be deprecated, as incompatible with the spirit
of the framers of our excellent Constitution. We
have no " Court Circle," nor do we expect to remain
a republic and at the same time ape " Court" manners.
America has a social as well as a political autonomy.
Let us preserve these with an equal jealous care and
dignity. Our official etiquette is not intended as a
personal compliment, but addresses itself to the office
borne ; so that it remains strictly ·in harmony with
our republican sentiments. When the incumbent
loses office he becomes again only a private citizen
whom the republic has honored. This is such a very
beautiful provision of our legal Constitution, that we
should never lose sight of its bearing on social life

and manners. It is the counteracting and saving element, as opposed to all hereditary distinction, and holds each man and woman intact in the exercise of those talents by which he or she may regulate the individual destiny. The very words " Republican Court " have a fatal sound of Cæsarism ; and, as has already been remarked, words become facts,—they are the expression of the soul's aspirations. We should prove to the world that republican manners are the very acme of true elegance in their unaffected simplicity.

It has always been, and still remains, a matter of discussion as to whom properly belongs the second place in social precedence, and equally accomplished persons differ on this point. This position is claimed for both the Chief Justice and the Vice-President, and so many good reasons may be given on either side that until a social congress can be convened to decide this and some other controverted points there can be no decision attained. It seems to us, however, that the Chief Justice exercises functions of such sacred importance and of such a nature that the second place should be given to him. He presides over the tribunal of ultimate appeal, he holds his office for life, he is placed beyond all the mutations incident to most other officials, however exalted. We have only to read the Constitution of the United States to be impressed with the immense dignity of his position, which he derives directly from the Con-

stitution.* The same immutability characterizes the
functions of the other Justices of the Supreme Court,
who hold their positions for life, and are placed on a
higher plane, and one above the political excitements
of the country. These gentlemen are to be respectively addressed in conversation as Mr. Chief Justice
and as Mr. Justice; and it has been usual to accord
them precedence over Cabinet Ministers and Senators,
for at times they may exercise a controlling influence
over the Executive. At least I have seen this precedence given, although one can recall, in our earlier
life, some bitter feuds on this score between the wives
of Court and Cabinet dignitaries, and I never yet
remember to have heard of a feminine warrior retreat-
ing when she once was committed to open battle. So
these ladies may have left a legacy of contested honors
to those who came after them. If so, in the name of
Heaven's first law, let us have peace.

If, then,—for we tread on shaking ground,—these
Justices walk in their silken robes so high, why not
give the Chief Justice precedence over the Vice-
President? And this I venture to suggest without
any derogation to the exalted position of the Vice-
President, whose chief dignity arises from his being
President of the United States Senate; for, as Vice-
President simply, he has no cares, no special duties,
no political significance. His political importance is

* See Hickey's *Constitution of the United States.* 12o.   John
Murphy & Co., Baltimore.

rather anticipatory than actual. Yet I must say that I would only rather avoid this difficulty at my own table by being careful not to invite these two high dignitaries to meet at the same time.

Succeeding the President, the Vice-President, the Chief Justice, comes the Speaker of the House. The power of the House of Representatives of the United States of America can scarcely be fully measured. It constitutes in fact, as well as in name, the great representative body of the supreme will of the sovereign people; and it gives an unerring expression of the public will, as derived directly from the popular choice. Therefore, the Presiding Officer, chosen by the House, represents a political influence of the first magnitude. He is emphatically the *Vox Populi.* Yet socially he comes in the fourth place. He is addressed in conversation as "Mr. Speaker." All these gentlemen I have mentioned receive the first visit from all others.

The General of the Army and the Admiral of the Navy, created after the late Civil War, occupied very exceptional positions. They filled stations made for them by a grateful country in recognition of special services, and the rank they held was bestowed upon them for life. Yet, properly speaking, they left no successors except as the roll of fame shall proclaim these trumpet-tongued to the nation. As to the social precedence their rank entitled them to, inasmuch as they moved, as it were, in eccentric orbits, they were

allowed the brilliant revolutions of luminaries which
appear in the heavens and disappear without inter-
ruption to the general plan; in plain words, they
were special creations, and not an essential part of
the machinery of the state, and left no successors
to their places. They came after the four classes
of officials I have mentioned, and, relatively to
each other, according to the order of the creation of the Army and Navy Departments by the
Government. This rank, it would seem, was theirs
by right, and not by courtesy alone, as the General
of the Army and the Admiral of the Navy represented the two arms of the Government through
whom it must act directly in case of war. Some are
of opinion that these special creations, whenever made,
should hold social positions of precedence subordinate
to the Cabinet and to the Senate. Regarding this, it
may be asked, To what dizzy height may the Senate,
expressing the acclaim of the nation, and vested with
the confirming power by the Constitution, raise those
whom they delight to honor? Does this august body
take these patriotic defenders of the republic from the
gates of the Temple of Janus, which these heroes have
closed, invest them with titles as with a shining rai-
ment, and, at the same moment, limit *their own power*
of conferring this lustre of renown? Does not the
very precedence which may be thus assigned them—
this place set apart by common consent, as in the case
of the Chief Magistracy—present the utmost possible

inducement the country may offer to stimulate military and naval achievement? Nor can the Senate be less in honor when it thus assists to build so high the bulwarks of the Executive in time of war; and it must not be overlooked, as has already been said, that no general rule can become established here, for at the death of the incumbents the stations disappear. It will then anew require the Promethean spark of *genius aiding opportunity* to revive the rank. Until such time may again come, the Army and Navy will once more be commanded by the Senior Officer of the service, and, routine resuming its sway, the old place under the respective Departments will be assigned.

Among officers of the Army and Navy there exists a corresponding or relative rank,—the General and the Admiral, the Lieutenant-General and the Vice-Admiral, the Major-General and the Rear-Admiral, the Brigadier-General and the Commodore, the Colonel of the Army relatively to the Captain of the Navy, and so on *pari passu.* Upon this rule a social precedence can alone be placed whenever formal or ceremonious occasions require it. In England the Navy has precedence over the Army, inasmuch, I suppose, as the British nation in the highest degree owes its grandeur and prosperity to the perfection of its naval power and to its commercial marine. Hence every possible incentive to aim at brilliant success is given by England to the Navy. But the American nation, considering the magnitude of its seaboard and interior seas, is strangely apathetic about granting the highest form of encouragement to naval achievement, and *social honor* is recognized the world over as the very culmination of success. In this matter, as in all others, the *political* uses dominate with us. , It is one of the vices of our system. The soldier *votes*, while the sailor at sea makes even *this* highest sacrifice of his "birthright" for his ungrateful country. And sometimes poor Jack does not receive his "mess of pottage" in return.

I have now to consider the Cabinet; and here I must remark that so much confusion at once appears as really to make the whole subject a discouraging one.

As to the Cabinet, relatively to each other, the order observed is that priority in which these offices were created,—thus: the State, the Treasury, the War, the Department of Justice, the General Post-Office, the Navy, the Interior and the Department of Agriculture. The chiefs of these Departments form the Executive Council of the Administration, but at the same time they are actual Heads of Departments of State. These functionaries alike expect to receive calls, and alike claim the same privileges; and it is only upon state occasions, such as official receptions, or formal state dinners, or other state ceremonials, that their order need be specially defined. Yet these situations are of not unfrequent occurrence, and no embarrassment should arise when they do present themselves.

It has been a contested point as to who should pay the first visit upon each other,—the Cabinet officer or the Senator,—but there would seem to be a growing tendency to yield to the Senatorial claim. This claim is based on the argument that the Senator represents State sovereignty, and that the dignity is, consequently, superior to that of the Cabinet officer, whose nomination the Senate confirms by its vote, and who is appointed constitutional aid and adviser of the President. Yet the Cabinet officer is something more than this; for, presiding over an entire Department of the Government, he possesses both power and dignity of function. As to his confirmation being subject to the vote of the Senate, the Senator, in turn, is subject to the State Legislature for his appointment, and this line of reasoning would place a State Senator above a United States Senator, and the Great Unwashed above the State Senator. Evidently, we cannot go back to first principles too closely in a republic in order to regulate our ceremonial.

The fact remains that it is the Constitution of the United States of America upon which our autonomy as a nation must rest, and which must be the underlying principle of all our laws, customs and social usages, as well as those peculiar adaptations that give us a national or distinctive character. This Constitution, while it would seem at first glance to be a marvel of simplicity, is really more complex, because taking a wider and deeper and higher range than any form of government on the face of the earth.

A despotic government voices but one will; a constitutional monarchy embodies the one man power under certain limitations; but our glorious Constitution, derived from a people for a people, combines all interests. Its series of adjustments are of such nice discrimination and delicate balance, that it would seem to require a special inspiration to properly adapt the complicated machinery of our social forms to this standard of the highest plane of the world's progress.

But I do not propose to enter the domain of constitutional law, but simply to explain points, some established and others controverted, of social law, and give reasons, where any exist, for certain customs.

The matter of relative precedence between the Cabinet and the Senate has, perhaps, been made somewhat more complicated by a statute approved January 19th, 1886, regulating what a strained phrase might designate as the Presidential succession. It reads thus :

"In case of removal, death, resignation or inability of both the President and Vice-President, a member of the Cabinet shall, in the following order, act as President until the disability is removed or a President elected : The Secretary of State, Secretary of the Treasury, Secretary of War, Attorney-General,

Postmaster-General, Secretary of the Navy, Secretary of the Interior : Provided, That whenever the powers and duties of the office of President of the United States shall devolve upon any of the persons named herein, if Congress be not then in session, or if it would not meet in accordance with law within twenty days thereafter, it shall be the duty of the person upon whom said powers and duties shall devolve to issue a proclamation convening Congress in extraordinary session, giving twenty days' notice of the time of meeting."

Subsequently another act was passed, simply adding the Secretary of Agriculture on the list of eligibilities, placing him at the foot.

It will be seen, upon a careful perusal of this statute, that it is so evidently intended only to fill an interregnum in 'case of possible accident to the two Chief Executive officers elected by the people ; that it can scarcely be claimed to invest the Cabinet officer with a special added weight of dignity. It is but an *ad-interim* measure of safety, while the real accession to the Presidency must come through a re-election.

The Chief Executive of this nation must be created by the people. We can but go back to this fountain head of honor; and, if we bear this cardinal principle well in mind, we cannot get bewildered. Thus this merely precautionary legislation leaves undisturbed the real relative significance of position, as between

3

the Cabinet and the Senate. On the other hand, there would seem to be too great a tendency in the Senatorial argument for precedency that gives undue weight to the idea that Senators represent sovereign States, and must be granted social rights in accordance with the majesty they represent.

It is conceded that this subject of State's rights is dangerous ground; and, as we have fought out and settled that claim as subordinated to the Union, it will be safest to hold all social precedence as a corollary founded thereon, well in abeyance. However, the great dignity of Senators, as the direct representatives of States, should not be overlooked. For, indeed, not a few of these States exceed in area, in wealth, and in the importance of their multiplied interests, the lesser nations of the earth.

To my apprehension, leaving grave Cabinet Ministers and Senators to arrange questions of relative social importance,—or rather their wives to do this for them, for it is women who are social agitators in the Republic,—one must really think that Senators' wives might safely yield this point to the Cabinet, when all the circumstances are considered; or, if this cannot be effected, at least let a compromise be made, that certain *privileges* are to be accorded by courtesy, still to be held in reserve as a *right*.

The ladies of the Cabinet have literally the public at their doors, and no one woman can possibly have health, strength and endurance to enable her to meet

the heavy burden imposed.   These ladies are few in
number, their residence here is fixed, central, and well
known, while the families of Senators often come here
for a short period of time only, and, unless they call
in person, or send their card giving their address, the
utmost vigilance may not detect their momentary presence.   It is true that many Senators have permanent
residences here also, and even live in a superior style
to Cabinet officers, yet one now speaks of the general
rule.   The rapidly-increasing size of our society really
demands that there should be some exemption allowed
by custom to the higher officers of the executive, with
regard to the personal notice of visits.   If it were
once understood that to return a call by a card sent,
and afterwards acknowledge the visit received (in all
cases where the person who calls has any social claims
that are recognized in general society) by cards of
invitation to receptions, these ladies would then be
allowed some respite.   To return a thousand visits in
person is a hardship none can realize except those who
have attempted the task.   And, moreover, it becomes
an utterly senseless formality.   Why are these calls
made by society in general ?   They are made as a
mark of respect for the elevated station, and also in
order to participate in the receptions which these
functionaries give from time to time.   These objects
could be better met if it were permissible to send
cards in recognition of visits, and if, where personal
visits were made, the exceptions simply included the

Supreme Court, the United States Senate, the Diplomatic Body, the General and the Admiral, while outside of these functionaries an exception was allowed; and, if *this rule* were once established, no invidious comments could be made. That which renders it so very disagreeable *now* to receive a card in place of a personal visit, is the knowledge that your call is not treated with the same respect that is paid to that of others; but a general rule could not produce ill-feeling. We see this notably in the case of the President and his wife. No one feels aggrieved because his or her visit is in no manner returned by these personages.

Again, the card receptions that Cabinet Ministers find it incumbent to give are of necessity so large that they are unpleasantly crowded for both host and guest. Why not select some suitable public hall for these receptions, and let each Cabinet Minister hold therein one, two or more card receptions during what is called "the season?" I know of no social experience so disagreeable as to make one of a dense mass of human beings literally packed into rooms of ordinary dimensions. It forms no compensation that it is the "polite world" that suffocates you! Let any one, philosophically or cynically disposed, gain, if he can, a few inches of space in a corner, and become a spectator of such scenes as occur every winter at our crowded receptions, and the sheer absurdity of calling this aggregation, social life becomes at once apparent. It is rather to be wondered at that dreadful accidents have not be-

fore now recalled society to its senses in this matter.
One may enter many a hospitable door, and, look-
ing upward, behold such a surging mass of human
beings on the stairway that, dismayed at the idea of
wedging one's self into this fearful crowd, wraps are
sent back into the carriage from the door, rather than
attempt to gain the dressing-room, and, only ventur-
ing far enough to pay respects to the beleaguered host
and hostess, one makes a speedy exit : society, conversation, beauty of effect, are all lost, all rendered
impossible, through want of space.

And this evil will go on increasing, unless some
changes are effected. It is said that the Cabinet of
the present administration, alarmed at the heavy bur-
dens borne by their predecessors, contemplate making
some change with regard to the personal return of
visits. But it would seem that any departure from
hitherto established usage *must be made by common
consent* to be well received or effective.

This change, doubtless, could be brought about if
the wives of all the leading functionaries of state
would publish a card defining their position in such
a way as to make it evident that no personal dis-
courtesy was intended, but rather the reverse. For
if physical strength can by any device be saved for
hospitable effort, the public is thereby better served.
Yet this is a most difficult and hazardous experi-
ment to make. The result would be that in some

cases a card would be left in reply to a personal
visit, while for others exceptions would be made.

The question arises at once—especially among
people of consideration who are not in official life,
and who would thus be overlooked—whether they
will consent to receive so partial an equivalent for
their visit. While it is not to be denied that official
life constitutes a leading element in Washington
society, yet the official, however brilliant, is after
all so very ephemeral that, in real solidity of social
importance, the resident society must always form
an essential feature, and be classed as of the very
élite.

Now, this resident society has reason to be jealous
of its privileges, for these are securely based upon
the highest respectability. The peculiar influences
and cosmopolitan atmosphere of the National Capital have given it refinement and breadth, which make
it too valuable an accessory to be overlooked. If
ladies whose husbands occupy official positions here
fail to recognize with due consideration the resident
social circle, it is to be feared that sufficient reason
will not exist to induce this society to add the charm
of its life-long training to their more transitory existence. Even in Paris, where the Minister rarely
makes a call in person, except upon his colleagues
or upon a representative of a foreign Power, yet if
the Minister wishes to accord particular respect to
eminent private worth, he does not hesitate to do so.

For instance, aged people of distinction or others of extraordinary merit may be called upon without any rule existing to prevent it. Certainly it is disagreeable to receive a card in return for a personal visit, and people of independent social position who have equal society favors to offer in exchange, will hesitate long and perhaps refuse entirely to subject themselves to such treatment.

The fact, however, cannot be overlooked that all of society in Washington who entertain much, suffer from the present custom of being expected to exchange visits in person. An emancipation, therefore, needed more or less by all, is the substitution of *exchange of cards for exchange of visits.* Such substitution would give more time and a fuller measure of strength for *an exchange of hospitality.* If we could ever claim this happy freedom, and an exemption be mutually accorded from the never-ceasing, never-ending, meaningless round of calls, society life in this city would reach its acmé. Then the personal visit could be limited to the recognition of invitations, or as a mark of personal regard, for special reasons. What an ocean of inane talk would be avoided ; what painful, irreparable loss of precious time saved !

No great importance can be attached to the momentary morning call, other than as the formal prelude to a better acquaintance at the social reunions they are intended to precede. If society would only consent to

assume that an exchange of cards was to be considered
as but a complimentary prelude to a higher exercise
of hospitality, the card would then be graciously received. Of course no one person will be allowed to
initiate such an innovation. Our social customs, like
our language, can only be altered in their polite uses
by that *common consent* that makes law.

If ever a woman's parliament ought to be convened,
it would be to relieve our social life in Washington
from the senseless waste of time involved in the tread-
mill routine of social visits. A clever woman, whom
I met making a round of reception visits, said, "You
do not *see* my chain, but I am a galley-slave none
the less!"

In the name of Liberty, who will arise to strike off
these shackles?

The same controversy as to the first visit, which
implies precedence, has always existed as regards the
Diplomatic Body, who represent other countries near
our own. I have known some ladies of the Senate
who have refrained from making the first visit upon
the wives of Foreign Ministers, assigning the same
reason, that the Senators represented a State sovereignty, while the Minister was only an accredited
functionary from a foreign power, it being held that
the Ambassador or Envoy alone properly represented
the sovereignty of a State.

Since the recent enactments by Congress, creating
the Ambassadorial rank, and the reciprocal action

of the several nations who have sent us Ambassadors to represent them, much confusion would seem to exist, as to the proper place in our social scale to assign these personages. Having made a serious departure from Jeffersonian simplicity, in making these creations, we are as a consequence met by the anomaly, which any deviation from strictly republican principles brings with it. Nor can we extricate ourselves from the illogical position we have assumed, by adopting any established order of precedence, existing abroad, because we are a Republic, and as such expressly disclaim the entire fabric of inherited distinctions and relative rank based upon class privileges. Our immortal forefathers broke asunder for us those enfolding cerements that constrain the living to a dead past.

Now it is important not only as regards Ambassadors, but also other members of the Diplomatic Body, that we should assign to these accredited Representatives and agents their exact place. Otherwise we incur the danger, that in the interests they represent, they will as a consequence of our failure take the matter in hand for themselves and designate to us where we are to place them, which would, to say the least, be a humiliation well deserved by us.

When we send an Ambassador or Minister, or other diplomatic agent to another country, they expect to take such place as shall be given them in the scale of precedence, wherever they may be accredited, and

surely a vast nation like ours cannot tolerate any
departure at our National Capital from this usage.
It is for us to designate to the foreigner in our midst
what our scale of precedence is. And the precedence
we are to recognize must be in conformity with our
own institutions. Strictly speaking, the only precedence we can tolerate must be of a representative
character and never individual. While abroad, precedence on the contrary defines principally the relative rank of the titled classes.

In England, as far back as 1339, such regulations
were officially issued, and during the reign of King
Henry VIII, Parliament by statutory enactments
took cognizance of the subject. Thus were their
titled classes hedged around and bulwarks built to
secure them in their assumptions and class privileges.
Would it be amiss if our Congress were to define
by enactment the relative representative place to be
given in state ceremonial? Inasmuch as such place
would be *representative and not individual,* it would
be in harmony with the National dignity and our
institutions, and serve as a protection against the
introduction of foreign customs, as well as the senseless invasions against republican forms of our pluto-
cratic ultra-fashionable ninnies.

As to the position to be assigned Ambassadors in
our social scale, a single extract from Burke's *Peerage*
will serve to show us that we must make a law for
ourselves, and cannot be guided in this matter by
foreign ceremonial.

Burke says : "Ambassadors yield precedence only to Members of the Royal family of the Court, to which they are accredited, and to the sons and brothers of Crowned Heads. Foreign Ministers and Envoys have no real claim to precedence. The question was raised and settled at the Congress of Vienna in 1815, but of late years place has been allowed them in this country, after Dukes and before Marquesses."

For those who may care to know the regulations adopted by the Congress of Vienna alluded to, I have given them in Appendix B, taken from Burke's *Peerage.* One may thus clearly see that certain considerations compatible with our own form of government must guide us, in assigning a place of relative dignity to the Diplomatic Body represented amongst us by Ambassadors and other accredited personages near our Government.

And, in the first place, the Ambassador, holding the representative place of a nation, may well be given a precedence over all functionaries, however exalted, except the President, the Vice-President, the Chief Justice and the Speaker. These enumerated high officials represent all that is most august in our nation, and typify the executive, the judicial and the legislative powers—that is, *the Nation.* The Cabinet, it is true, are socially of the family of the President, but this is not a class distinction, nor can it be said to give any claim comparable in any way to that of

the representative character, which we can alone take
cognizance of, and which belongs to the four high
officials we have enumerated and also to all the Justices of the Supreme Court, as well as the Senators
who represent States.

But having placed Ambassadors upon so high a
pinnacle, because of their representative character as
regards nations, the Justices of the Supreme Court,
the Senators and the members of the Cabinet are
each and all entitled to their respective places of relative precedence as regards the rest of the Diplomatic
Corps near this Government.

Among the Ambassadors themselves, relatively to
each other, priority gives the precedence. It must
likewise be borne in mind that whatever titles are
held by foreigners in our midst confer by right no
rank with us. Whatever deference we consent to
yield in this direction is simply an obliging civility
on our part. But having fearlessly asserted the cour-
age of one's convictions as a logical sequence of the
inherent grandeur of our principles and the broad
democracy of our social customs as far outweighing
all class distinctions as such, I would make an
urgent appeal, in behalf of the foreigner, *of courtesy
to the stranger.*

Courtesy is the flower of culture, the expression of
the highest refinement, and like hospitality ennobles
those who extend it. It is not a form, but a virtue.
Based upon this sentiment, which should prevail in

their case, I would grant a Foreign Minister the extent of precedence which can be given with any measure of propriety or of respect for our own institutions. Their place relatively to each other, rank being equal, is accorded to priority of residence among us. The *Dean* or *Doyen* enters upon his functions in virtue of length of stay near our Government. Yet I have witnessed very grave offence given at a dinner-table, where the host led in the wife of a Foreign Minister, the fair belligerent being the wife of a Senator who claimed the honor as her due.

Now, since it is to be presumed that the special object of every entertainment is to promote good will and not to foster ill-will, it is to be regretted that the rule that defines social-official classification is not more definite. A carefully adjusted ceremonial would be no more incompatible with republican institutions than the legal classification which now exists, and which must continue to endure. These have a fixedness coexistent with the republic, and our social life is their complement. Let us not undervalue its importance. Daniel Webster called a well-appointed dinner "the climax of civilization." We ought to be able to reach this climax smoothly. The breakfast, the luncheon, the five-o'clock tea, the "*matinée dansante*," the *musicale*, the *soirée* and the assembly are all and each charming in their degree as adjuncts of social life, yet the dinner is "*the climax.*"

Now, there are some dinner rules which are absolute, although I fear at times they are either misunderstood or at all events disregarded. It seems needless to recapitulate; and yet the very fact that mistakes are so often made must serve as an apology here. For instance, an invitation to dine must be precise, and should be couched in some such formula as the following:

MR. JONES

REQUESTS THE HONOR OF

MR. SMITH'S

COMPANY AT DINNER

On Monday, the 1st December, at 7 o'clock.

Nov. 22, '93.

When such an invitation is received, an answer should not only be given in writing, but it should be sent at the very earliest moment at all practicable.

I knew a diplomat here, renowned for courtly manners and for the incomparable dinners which he gave, whose answer to a dinner invitation came on one occasion so promptly that my own messenger, who also returned quickly, had not reached the house when the acceptance arrived. And the fine point on this piece of good manners was that this was an acceptance, not a regret, which is considered to demand greater expedition even in the sending. This gentleman entertained his friends so constantly at dinner that he understood the importance of prompt attention. In writing an answer to a formal dinner invitation, one should be careful to make it as exact as the note one has received. Indeed, this note should be repeated. If the host has a title,—for instance, The President,—repeat his title just as he himself may indicate to you. In answer to Mr. Jones, you reply:

MR. SMITH

HAS THE HONOR TO ACCEPT

MR. JONES'

KIND INVITATION TO DINNER

For Monday, the 1st December, at 7 o'clock.

Nov. 22, '93.

The reason for this repetition is to show that you have perfectly comprehended the invitation, so that no error may have been committed as to time or place.

I have known awkward mistakes to occur from want of attention in this matter.

Then, again, there should be no possibility of mistake as to your acceptance or non-acceptance. Let your answer be positively "Yes" or "No." At any other entertainment we may perhaps avail ourselves of a reasonable uncertainty, but not so with the dinner.

I once knew a poor little lady, "on hospitable thoughts intent," who went to live in a small town in the West. She had been accustomed to the well-regulated dinner at home, and had been taught to consider that the highest form of compliment was to ask a friend to dinner. Wishing to be on the best terms with her new neighbors, she sent out the usual written cards of invitation to a score of guests,—a formidable undertaking in a country village,—but she was in no wise daunted, and all the preparations went on bravely. Everything bade fair to make her dinner a success, except the dreadful fact that up to the very last moment she remained uncertain as to the number of her guests. In reply to her written invitations came a score of *verbal* messages, such as; "They *hoped* to come;" "Would come if they could;" "Could not tell *exactly* if their engagements would permit;" "If well enough, would come." But in no one case was a positive response received. So the banquet had to be prepared on this score. The hour came and passed, and, after a famishing delay which spoiled everything, two tardy guests dropped straggling in, and four rueful people sat down to a superb dinner prepared for twenty covers. This actually took place.

This grand collapse is just what may be expected where no one knows his own intentions, and society would receive its final doom did such conditions widely exist. Yet very disagreeable complications have arisen, even in Washington, from not paying due attention to the importance of a *definite answer*. Suppose, for example, there are *fourteen* covers at your dinner; and fourteen forms a pleasant and favorite number, suiting very well the size of the home dining-room ordinarily. Let fourteen be all counted, and suppose one guest disappoints! He leaves *thirteen* miserable souls to tell ghost-stories and wonder if the dinner will poison them, which very likely it may do, since they were all so "blue" in the discussing of it. It must be remembered that the guests at a dinner-table must be properly placed in advance, each plate marked with the name of the expected guest written on a card, or on the *menu*, or bill of fare, and the *dinner chart* mapped out, as if by line and compass, so as to avoid all these sunken rocks and breakers I have been considering, so as to place people who will like each other in proximity, so as to give "honor where honor is due," so as to keep husband and wife from treading on each other's toes, so as to please those you entertain by giving widows and marriageable young ladies desirable "*partis*" to captivate, so as to put the decanter of old Madeira near the *bon-vivant*, so as to leave the ends of your table open and unoccupied

4

and the central places filled with your most distinguished guests. Now, how is all this, and more too,
to be done—pleasure to reign, confusion to be avoided,
exact distribution of this cornucopia of blessings to
be showered on your blissful guests—unless there
is *certainty?* Is not life miserable because of the
uncertainty of all its enjoyments, and are we thus
ever to be cheated of even momentary happiness?
A thousand times, say yes or no, and let the pleasure
of this supreme social gratification be unimpaired!

The length of time preceding the dinner invitation
marks the degree of formality which it is expected
will characterize the arrangements. A card of invitation sent three weeks in advance informs us of a
state dinner. Ten days of notification is the usual
time; after that even four or five days may be allowed,
as simply inviting to a social dinner, or even two
or three days if "*en petit comité.*" I once had the
honor to be "one of seven" at such a dinner, where
Seward, Stanton, and a foreign celebrity were entertained by a diplomat, the short stay in the city of
the guest of the occasion, whom we were invited
to meet, being the reason mentioned for the hurried
summons. But the informal dinner is rather the
privilege of private life, and one is now considering the official etiquette of Washington, where state
functionaries are expected to invite three weeks in
advance. To allow so much time is certainly the
highest compliment, since it more surely secures the

original number selected. The time designated having arrived, *punctuality* is imperative. Dinner rules
do not allow over fifteen, or at the most twenty,
minutes of delay, in order to await the arrival of
any guest, no matter how exalted his functions in
the State may be. Courtesy to those present requires
that you give the company assembled their dinner
before it spoils or grows cold. So pray arrive, if
you can, at the precise moment at which you are
invited. If you reach the house the first guest at a
dinner, in place of waiting until some one else shall
appear, rather pride yourself upon your superior good
breeding for the nonce, and enter at once. Ladies
attend formal dinners "*en grande toilette,*" or "full
dress," and gentlemen in the corresponding and conventional dress suit of black, with white "choker,"
—only, messieurs, do not wear *white* gloves; take
lavender or any delicate tint in preference. At times
officers of the army or navy prefer to show their
respect by appearing in uniform; and one loves this
dress so well—it appeals so gratefully to patriot-
ism—that one is always glad to see it. Yet senior
officers especially, having been "in harness," as these
old "war-horses" call it, all their lives, are not sorry
to get rid of the constraint and wear the dress suit
of black also. However, if the occasion is one of
state, this will scarcely be permitted. Gloves must be
worn upon entrance to the drawing-room, but must
always be taken off at the moment one is seated at the

table. A recent innovation, which, if the fashionable
world could suspect was *an economy*, would probably
be at once scouted, but which I like *anyway*, per-
mits that the gloves shall not be replaced at all after
their removal at the table. This, however, may be
only one of those flitting fashions, worn like the glove
for the moment, and then cast aside. Yet do not forget that during the serving of a dinner the waiters in
attendance *alone* wear gloves! And even the waiter
serves with greater elegance with the thumb of the
hand wrapped in a damask napkin. Previous to
the announcement that "dinner is served," the host
informs each gentleman which lady he is expected to
lead in to dinner, and introduces them to each other
in case they happen not to be acquainted. Indeed,
I think at a dinner of moderate size the *convives*
should all know each other, and should be introduced,
if need be, by the host. Dinner announced, the host
offers his left arm to the lady who has the highest
official position present, and the hostess leaves the
drawing-room last, led in by the gentleman of the
first official distinction present. On leaving the table,
this order is reversed, the hostess leading the way.
I once knew of a lawless old diplomat who *would*
lead in with the prettiest young girl of the company
at his own splendid dinners; but his demoralizing -
course met that grave reprobation it deserved from
all virtuous matrons! As a just punishment for such
discreditable conduct, he fell a victim finally to an

innocent and confiding young creature of seventeen, left the country, and took his American bride to his foreign home, where he lives doubtless a reformed man, if indeed he still survive!

Thus our polite host and hostess take the central seats opposite to each other, being supported on either side by their most distinguished guests. The reason the extreme ends of a table should be left open, no seats placed there if possible, and at all events never occupied by the entertainers, is very obvious; since from a central position one can better care for one's guests, and promote conversation and a genial and measured degree of hilarity; while on the other hand, if guests are given the extreme ends, it may seem to place them "below the salt." Courtesy to the hostess requires that the guests, upon being assigned to their places, should remain standing until she is seated. Then the ladies are seated next; afterwards their escorts place themselves. As to the suitable service of a table, Washington has many good caterers and intelligent waiters, whose attendance can readily be procured, in case the home establishment needs to be reinforced—as indeed it generally does—in order to meet the requirements of a banquet. So the chief care of the host and hostess should be to forget that the dinner is being served, and try to interest their guests. As to the *menu*, or bill of fare, which it is better to put at each plate, for the information of the epicurean appetite, I would suggest not to yield

implicitly to the caterer, who will be sure to prolong
your dinner beyond the bounds of good taste. Especially should this be the case where a sudden acqui-
sition of fortune gives hospitable people the means
of entertaining. Such persons, quite unaccustomed
to judge for themselves of what is really proper, are
readily imposed upon by those whose interest it is to
provide lavish feasts. A banquet must be sumptuous rather in the careful choice and quality than in
the profuse quantity of the selected dishes. If you
desire to spend money without stint when giving
dinners, do so rather by the artistic elaboration of
that which you present than by an endless repetition
of courses which pall upon the taste. Do not be
persuaded to exceed ten courses—it is wearisome;
let the wines be delicate, and do not mix wines in
which tastes conflict. The French custom (and the
French are unrivalled in all matters of taste) of only
presenting each wine once is excellent; it effectually
prevents all inebriating excess, which is so utterly
disgraceful if it happen to occur.

A very great reform, however, has taken place in
the past few years with regard to the use of wines.
Doubtless the agitation kept up by temperance societies has had something to do with this; but much
also has been effected by the happy introduction of
light native wines among us at moderate prices.
When the *vin-du-pays* becomes as cheap here as it is
in France or Italy, we shall have effectually swept

away the intoxicating poisons which as yet are demanded. I recollect hearing my father, the Hon. S. F. Vinton, say that when he came here in 1823, the then youngest member of the House, and a bachelor, he absolutely dreaded a dinner, on account of the social tyranny in the matter of drinking. Old English customs then prevailed at the dinner, and the calibre of a man's brain was measured at dinner by the capacity of his stomach to guzzle bumpers. For a man of exceedingly delicate nerve organization, such as Mr. Vinton had, who considered a clear head as absolutely needful for a wise legislator, this custom was torture. Let us rejoice that this enforced dissipation has given way to more Christian ideas. If we could only, when we exercise hospitality, learn to set aside such lavish luxury as sinful, and share with the poor of the Lord by dividing this excess somewhat with them, we would in this way, if only in an imperfect degree, obey the injunction to call in from the highways and the by-ways the suffering multitude. As I write of costly banquets my pen falters, and tearful visions of pale faces and of starving children rise before me. As a Christian woman, and as one hopes for mercy hereafter, I can but implore society to let the crumbs that fall from its table console the Lazarus at its door. Winter is always a time of unusual hardship for these little children of our common Father, and it would be well if some united action

could be had to avoid waste. But one turns the
saddened eye from the cold and chill and hungry
gaze without, to the light and warmth and glow
within, and again asks our pleasant hostess not to
be afraid of exercising her own individual taste in
the matter of adornment of her table. An original
thought, if it is graceful, pleases the old diner-out,
who wearies of the monotony of conventional elegance. It is too tiresome to see the same hired
ornaments day after day, and to go through the
same unvarying routine. Rather use a simple vase
of flowers than a piece of finery hired for the occasion. Personal care bestowed is more flattering than
the hired glitter. I once said to my hostess, "You
have produced a fine effect," when I was shocked
by the disclaimer, "And yet we took no pains."
Now, it was for this very "pains," for the thought-
ful care to please, that one thanked her.

Our dinner talk is over, the hostess rises first,
and all proceed to the drawing-room, where coffee,
the *demie-tasse*, cordials, and, an hour latter, tea are
served. The hostess usually serves the tea herself,
but this is not *de rigueur;* and although one loves to
see a hostess exercise " *les petits soins*,"—those little
acts of hospitable care,—yet I confess to being most
bent upon conversation, and to a dislike of anything
that interrupts the "feast of reason and the flow of
soul." The after-dinner hour is precious in its genial
exercise of intellect or for music. At such times a

gracious play of fancy is stimulated, and even the cup
of tea should be used " to cheer," and not to interfere.
Yet many a gentle dame presides so gracefully at the
tea-board, and dispenses the grateful beverage with
such pleasant words, that none may cavil. I have in
recollection now, one of our most honored matrons,
her placid face almost hidden by the burnished sil-
ver, the hissing tea-urn, the snowy bowl of sugar,
and as she handles the quaint old china I hear
her say, " For twenty-five years have I made tea,
seated just here, at this board,"—just twenty-five
years! And "here," then, the monarchs of thought,
who have toiled to bring about the culmination of
our nation's grandeur, have sipped their Bohea.
The " old families " of Washington have an interest
which none other in the land may claim, for their
social life has gone hand in hand with that of the
nation. But one has not yet bade the hostess adieu,—
a formality one may dispense with at a *soirée*, but not
at a dinner.

The gentlemen, some of them, are still in the smok-
ing-room. I feel sorry that they smoke so long, for
charming women are here, and it is the common loss.
Perhaps, like social cowards, they retreat from an
apprehended captivity.

One is at liberty to leave after the coffee, but the
guests linger still and sip their tea. However, during
what is called the season, social festivities become so
multiplied that one may have several engagements to

meet later than the dinner. It is therefore admissible
to leave as soon as the coffee is handed. Succeeding
the dinner a visit, which the French wittily call *visite
de digestion*, must be made within the week. While
descanting on dinner-table topics and of entertainments in general, I would strive anew to call attention to some finer points too often misunderstood. In
the first place, let it be held as a cardinal principle
that a mere outlay of money, unless directed by refinement of taste, can never attain successful results. The
dinners that marked the era of the Cæsars, the banquets, for instance, of Nero and of Caligula, have
scarcely, if ever, been equalled through the succeeding ages in lavish expenditure. The gastronomic
excesses of Pagan days, when thousands of dollars
were spent upon a single dish, were followed by the
sumptuous feasts of the Middle Ages, during which
the perfumed air, delicious strains of music, and an
infinitude of fanciful conceits were intended to captivate and enthrall the senses.

The barbaric glitter of these entertainments has
been in turn succeeded by a higher civilization,
which calls for something more than gastronomic
chefs-d'œuvre, and aims to promote festive wit. To
secure this end the first consideration must be a careful choice of guests. No dinner, however superb in
prandial show, can be agreeable if the *convives* are
dullards. If perfection is sought for, let the guests
and the courses not exceed the Muses in number.

No sordid computation of dollars can buy or measure the Promethean light of conversational effect. The "glad circle," then, must have this highest requisite. When music is introduced as an accessory, it should not be *bruyante*, but must be placed at such distance as to form, as it were, an undertone to the dinner-table talk, mingling with, harmonizing, but never overpowering, its effect. This is the true musical province of an *accompaniment*.

Avoid the growing taste for dining your friends at a club-house or outside of your own house. There is no savor of hospitality of so fine flavor as that of bringing your friends into your own home. Nothing can replace the Lares and Penates. Even the heathen understood this. Strive to individualize the style of your dinner, so as to give the zest of "something new" to its elegance. In this connection the artistic hand-painted *menus* and dinner-cards now so much in vogue are to be commended. One would also like to see more originality in the floral decorations of the dinner-table. This ornamentation is often more elaborate than tasteful. The poets sing to us of the "*language* of flowers." Why not speak to each guest in this style of graceful compliment? If the china merchants, stationers or other similar dealers would furnish *alphabetical forms in grooves*, to be filled in and hidden from sight by flowers, we could thus express with these *floral letters* ideas which would produce a new and pleasing variety.

Precedence at the dinner-table is the grand subject of social wrangling in Washington, and the need of a fixed rule is here so painfully apparent that those who have been taught to be careful by sad experience, will simply avoid asking those functionaries to meet each other whose claims may conflict. Yet the Vice-President, the Chief Justice, the Speaker, the General of the Army, the Admiral of the Navy, Ambassadors, Foreign Ministers, Cabinet Ministers and Senators, they and their wives, ought to be able to meet and dine in peace together. Let a social congress or woman's parliament be convened, composed of these ladies, where, after all the arguments and respective claims have been duly weighed, some positive rules may be agreed upon. It is surprising what *natural aristocrats* women are. In the army and navy, for example, the wives of officers adhere more rigidly to designated and relative social rank than the officers do themselves; nor do our American women object to bear foreign titles of distinction. Indeed, in this they reason wisely, in case they are so unfortunate as to leave their native land, for in countries where class distinctions exist, these usually *imply respectable lineage.*

I would here remark that Cabinet officers are addressed as " Mr. Secretary." I do not like this, for it designates the lowest rather than the highest functions which these officials fill. They are in one sense "secretaries" of the President, appointed by

the Executive head and confirmed by the United
States Senate; but at the same time they are active,
if not responsible, heads of vast departments of the
Government, with a power, patronage and influence
which, if it were permanent, would exceed that of
many petty potentates of other countries. *Names
become things* in history, and I believe if "Mr.
Secretary" were changed to "Mr. Minister," "The
Premier," and so on, it would help to adjust the
matter of social precedence.

Senators are addressed as "Mr. Senator," and this
is as it should be. Members of the House of Representatives are introduced as the "Honorable Mr.,"
but simply addressed in conversation as "Mr.," that
is, if a plain Mister can be found in that popular
body. But I venture to say, from an intimate
knowledge of our rural districts, that every man of
them bears *a title* at home. He is "Squire," "Judge,"
"Captain," "Colonel," "General," and so through
all the gamut of the key-board of possible or impossible prefixes! The republic seems to avenge
itself for having made the permanency of families
unattainable, by piling Pelion upon Ossa during a
man's natural life! And now come women who
claim to be Miss Doctor and Mrs. Reverend on their
own account!

With regard to women's titles, it is becoming
more and more the custom to say "Mrs. Secretary,"
"Mrs. Senator," "Mrs. General," "Mrs. Admiral,"

and so on. They do this in Europe, to be sure, so
that it cannot be laughed at as ridiculous. Yet,
since we are a republic, we are supposed to stand on
the basis of personal merit and distinction won for
ourselves. But perhaps when a woman captures a
President or other dignitary, she has won the right
to claim the title too. Some are said to " wear the
breeches," "rule the roast," be the "better half," and
" captain of the ship." From my own observation
at the Capital of this great nation, something more
of substance than the empty title is wielded by the
women who represent the country here. And I
should be very sorry to see our fair and very able
sisters disturbed in their privileges and right womanly
prerogatives. How much nicer, for example, to be
the wife of a President than to be Mr. President!
for, as it is, one has a good share of the power and
none of the responsibility. But of course one don't
mean exactly what one says : women often do not.
I think, however, that while it may be in good
taste to give a lady these titular distinctions, held
really by their husbands, yet it would be in bad
taste to use them for one's self. Certainly it is very
convenient, when introducing ladies, to give such
nominal rank as may at once clearly and distinctly
designate them in the very fact of introduction. It
would often save a long explanation, or an uncertainty still more disagreeable.

In England, Dowager Peeresses and titled widows take precedence of the wives of existing Peers of the same dignity. I think *the principle* upon which such respect is based is just and compatible with republican institutions. It would in this republic be but a grateful and proper recognition, whenever pre-eminent service to the nation is given, that the widows of such patriots of distinction should be assigned a place of honor and dignity. Such recognition would also form an additional incentive to its citizens to serve their country with exceptional diligence and ability.

Members of the House of Representatives and their wives are expected to make the first visit upon all classes of functionaries mentioned; but citizens of Washington, and those in private life, owe them in turn the first visit.

There is a form of government in this city, but one really can have no idea of what its social claims may be; but it would seem, as compared to the National Government, that it must stand as a separate creation and take a subordinate position. Perhaps the Commissioner's office may be exceptional to this rule.

If this mode of government continue in existence, those who write on this theme ten years hence will be able to judge better. Yet, thus far, everything connected with the management of this District has been subject to so various change that we can only exclaim, *Omne principium grave!*

The citizens of Washington form among themselves, outside of the consideration of official life, a
body of society to be regulated by the same rules
which dominate other societies; yet, as I have said
before, Washington life is essentially official life, and
one can scarcely separate the two.

When you attend a reception, do not omit to leave
your card with the usher in the hall. In some houses
it is the custom always to give your name to the
usher, who then announces you à *haute voix*. Of
course, in a society where so many strangers meet,
and which is so cosmopolitan in its nature, it may
often be essential to announce in this way. In public
receptions it is entirely so; but a protest must be
entered against the awkward usher who murders your
name outright, cuts you into halves, and shows you
no quarters. As to those foreigners who have a
quartering to their names, they must be fearful suf-
ferers! Let the usher be well trained to announce,
or dispense with his services in this respect altogether, as an unmitigated nuisance. A gentleman
of distinction once came into my drawing-room with
a sigh of relief as I greeted him by the well-known
cognomen.

"How good it is," said he, "to hear my name
once more! I began to be uncertain as to my own
identity."

I laughed, and asked what he meant. "Well,
simply this: I have been attending receptions all the

morning, and have heard my name so mangled by the ushers, and have found myself repeated under so many different titles, that I am bewildered."

Use a plain card, if you do not wish to be supposed fanciful; and never have it printed. Great men, whose autographs are precious, confer a favor certainly by writing the name on the card, but it is more convenient and more elegant for society in general to have the name engraved on the card. It is also very comfortable for old ladies who read through glasses if these letters are plain and legible.

The clergy take a signal position, and should always be accorded *the* place of honor when present in society. They are Envoys of a Higher Power, and have the most important and sacred mission of all. I was once at a dinner where a clergyman was present, and there were Foreign Ministers and Cabinet Ministers, Senators, and others of dignity, when the venerable *Doyen* of the Corps Diplomatique asked the hostess to assign the place at her side, for which he had been designated, to the clergyman. And this wise old gentleman, who understood so well all matters of social courtesy, decided on true principles based upon that Divine law which is above human law and goes beyond it. In England, Archbishops rank with Dukes. A similar, or a greater, appreciation for the clergy is everywhere held as of polite usage.

Very aged persons, also, should be treated with peculiar respect. God has stamped upon them the

5

majesty of years, and we must give them a deferential place. Some years ago the nation beheld a touching example of filial respect in the family of its Chief Magistrate, and it was a providential spectacle at a time when insubordination to parents is a growing evil throughout the land. Many years since, a friend, the wife of a public man, was led in to dinner by the then President. The aged father of His Excellency being present, it was made a question if the President should precede his own father. *By right* as President, yes; by filial courtesy as a son, no. The nation is fortunate to have repeated the beautiful lesson of filial affection for its example. Exceptions to ordinary claims of social or even official precedence may also be allowed by courtesy to strangers of distinction who make us passing visits, to remarkable worth and merit, such as philanthropists and other benefactors of mankind exhibit, or to extraordinary and acknowledged scientific, artistic, or literary excellence. Deference to these conditions illustrates the existence of that advanced state of civilization which it is our aim to acquire.

In making visits always send in or leave your card. . At receptions the usher takes your card. At other times the person called upon not being at home, you turn down the right-hand upper corner of the pasteboard to indicate that you came in person ; and if the visit is intended for the various members of a family, you either give several cards or leave one

with the entire right side folded over. The choice
is immaterial. When you go away from the city
altogether, do not omit to send a card upon which
P. P. C. is written on the right-hand lower corner,
and if this visit of *adieu* is made in person turn down
the right-hand lower corner. A prompt notice should
be taken of the first visit received, and when such visit
inaugurates an acquaintance, the card or call should be
at once honored. An intervening period not exceed-
ing three days marks high breeding, as it evinces your
pleasure at forming the acquaintance, so that a return
visit within a day or so is therefore a delicate compliment. Dignitaries of state should make *instant* return
of the first visit. This also is navy etiquette. With
regard to entertainments other than the dinner, one
is at liberty not to send a written answer of acceptance; but in case of non-acceptance it is certainly
more polite to send a regret. Of course, if an
answer is requested (the R. S. V. P. means the
same thing) an answer should be given accordingly.
When one has a small house it is important to know
what number of guests may be expected, and always
more pleasant for a hostess to be thus assured. In
making calls the usual visiting hours are from three
until six. This portion of the day is particularly
set apart for formal calls. An evening visit implies
some degree of social acquaintance, and should never
be made as a first call, unless you are invited to come
unceremoniously. A call of condolence should always

be made on occasions of death in the family of an acquaintance. Turn down the left-hand lower corner of the card.

Persons in private life, having no official position in Washington, are in a measure exempt from the necessity of making the official round of visits or of giving large entertainments; yet any one who enters into general society here must, of course, conform to the official rules of precedence and etiquette. Private life here has its advantages as well as its disadvantages. It is pleasant to select your own company, even though choice extends to but a limited number; and the private citizen is free to do this. Washington will certainly become more and more a central social point of attraction to persons of wealth and refinement who can exercise freedom of selection, and who will also add to the already charming variety of society. Such persons must surely appreciate our social advantages over all other cities of the Union.

Young people amongst us have never as a common rule been allowed to tyrannize over society as they do in New York and in other cities; and the ineffable vulgarity of *coteries* presided over by young ladies, and not dignified by the presence of their seniors, has not had much if any encouragement here. Probably the presence of so many personages of importance in the State, assists to keep the young in their proper place. One may here see, what is not so usual elsewhere, young ladies remain standing, as they should do, until the mother or married lady may be seated, and at all events an appearance of subordination which speaks well for the future. Formerly young people were not often invited to dinners, but left to participate in the simpler forms of gayety. It has been said that a woman did not enjoy a dinner-conversation, or play a good hand at whist, under thirty!

On New-Year's day ladies are not expected to make visits. Gentlemen call to pay the compliments of the season, and ladies stay at home to welcome visitors. However, this custom is falling into disuse.

I think our ladies make a mistake, and also fatigue themselves unnecessarily, by receiving standing. This is a great tax on the strength, and much more formal than is apt to be agreeable. In very large receptions a lady who receives can scarcely be seated; but in the usual morning at home would not our guests remain longer, and be more at ease, if seated in pleasant circles, rather than left standing in formal groups in the middle of the room? Magnetism counts for something the world over, and stiff constraint destroys electric currents.

As to the refreshments proper to provide at a morning reception, the choice is quite optional here, as in other of our cities.

The idea of writing this little pamphlet was first suggested by a distinguished personage here, who thought something of the kind would be well

received and ought to be published. The very limited scope I have given myself shows for itself
in the size of this little essay; for I have not pro-
posed to attempt the history of social customs since
pre-Adamitic periods, nor yet to instruct in all the
rules of a manual of good manners, nor to give the
rounded polish of a Chesterfield, but simply to indicate certain peculiarities of Washington society.

I have heard some of the subjects which have
just been hinted at, commented upon from my first
acquaintance with official social life here; and
although I have alluded to many little matters
which must seem rather puerile and perhaps un-
worthy of serious attention, yet these are the very
questions one asks most often upon first arrival in
Washington. I do not endeavor or presume to
instruct, but rather desire to recapitulate mooted
points, show how troublesome their unsettled con-
dition makes them, and ask for a woman's congress,
or "kitchen cabinet," or a statutory enactment to
define them in the interest of society.

So far as have been noted some customs, I have
preferred to leave as many more unnoted, on the
supposition that the reader forms a "court that
knows something."

Appendix A.

AS far back as 1825 the President held a levee every other Wednesday evening, and it was customary to make the announcement in the *National Intelligencer.* The hour was at that time from 8 to 10 P. M., and it was usual to offer some refreshments, which were placed on trays, and carried about the rooms by waiters. Gentlemen then appeared in small-clothes, which was the accepted full dress of the period; and I remember hearing my father say, that so great was the precision that, although some gentlemen occasionally wore boots, it was considered more proper to go in silk stockings and pumps. Of course the usual dress suit of black has long since taken the place of this more courtly, though less convenient, style of dress. It was not at first the custom to have music, except on New-Year's day, when a government band discoursed patriotic airs; but in the time of Mr. Adams, and after the East Room was opened, in 1828, music and dancing enlivened these receptions, and splendid suppers were given. So long as such degree of exact form marked these receptions as to assure only the

71

presence of well-bred people of decorous manners, this style of entertainment prevailed; but finally such excesses took place in the greater latitude that was afterwards allowed, as to make it unadvisable either to have dancing or to give suppers, except at invited entertainments; but of these, I remember some very memorable and elegant receptions that have been given, on special occasions, at the Executive Mansion.

I desire to append the following letter from John Quincy Adams, written when Secretary of State, and addressed as a private communication to the Vice-President of the United States. It strikes me that the eminent writer is somewhat illogical when he speaks of the "whole affair" as "of very little importance," while at the same moment he shows by the very subject-matter of his letter the "importance" then, as now, of adopting some more fixed and exact code. Until this is done, it will become more and more difficult to avoid misconstructions and unpleasant relations in a state of society where the social intercourse cannot be separated from official position and its exigencies. Even the public service requires this.

WASHINGTON, DEC. 29, 1819.

The Vice-President of the United States:

DEAR SIR,—It has been suggested to me, that some of the members of the Senate, entertaining the opinion that a formal visit in person or by card is due from each of the executive departments, at the commencement of every session of Congress, to every Senator upon his arrival at the seat of government, have considered the omission on my part to pay such visits as the withholding from them of a proper mark of respect, or even as implying a pretension to exact such a formality from them. Disclaiming every such pretension and every such claim on my part, I take the liberty of submitting to you the following explanation of the motives which have governed my conduct in relation to this subject.

I have invariably considered the Government of the United States as a Government for the transaction of business and that no ceremonial for the mode or order of interchanging visits between the persons belonging to the respective departments in it had ever been established. I was myself five years a member of the Senate, and at four of the five sessions of Congress which I attended was accompanied at this place by my wife. During that time I never once received a first visit from any one of the heads of departments, nor did my wife ever receive a first visit from any one of their ladies, except perhaps *once*, when she was sick, from Mrs. Madison We always called upon them soon after our arrival at Washington, not from any opinion that it was an obligation of duty, but because we understood and believed it to be usual, and because we did not think it improper. We made an exception, after the first session, with regard to Mr. Gallatin, who, never having returned my first visit, was supposed not to incline to that sort of intercourse with us.

When I came to reside at this place, two years since, I was under the impression that the usages, with regard to visiting, were as I had known and practised them ten years before,—that, as a member of the administration, I had no sort of claim to a first visit from any member of either house of Congress, but that neither had any member of Congress any claim to a first visit from me, that the interchange and order of visits was entirely optional on both sides, and that no rule of etiquette whatsoever existed which required that either party should pay the first visit, or indeed any visit, to the other.

In the course of the winter of 1817-18, two members of the Senate, for both of whom I entertained the highest respect, and with one of whom I had the pleasure of sitting several years in the Senate, called at my office, and informed me that there was a minute of a rule agreed upon, not officially but privately, by the members of the Senate of the first Congress, that the Senators of the United States paid the first visit to no person except the President of the United States. I observed to them that, as during five years' service as a Senator I had never seen or heard of this rule. I could hardly consider it as having been much observed; that I could, however, have no possible objection to the Senators prescribing to *themselves* any rule of visiting which they might think proper. But I asked them if they understood the rule as implying an order that *other persons* should first visit them? They answered, if I recollect right, By'no means. And I suppose they viewed the whole affair as I did,—that is, of very little importance. I have, therefore, paid no visits of form to members of the Senate; and, although always happy to receive and return the visits of those who please to call upon me, and happy to invite to my house every member of the Senate, whether he had or had not paid me a visit, who would give me the honor of his company, I yet always respected the motives of those who declined paying me any visit, or even frequenting my house at all. I exacted nothing from them which they might think incompatible with their dignity. I presumed they would exact nothing from me not within the line of my official duty. I soon learned that, if I should make it a rule to pay the first visit to every Senator at each session, the same compliment would be claimed, if not by all, at least by a large proportion of the members of the House of Representatives; and I could find no republican principle which would, to my own mind, justify me in refusing to the members of one house that which I should yield as due to the members of another. At the commencement of each session I have visited the presiding member of each house, not from a sense of obligation, but of propriety. I have not felt it my duty to pay first visits to any individual member of either house; nor has it entered my imagination that a first visit was *due* from any member of either house to me.

If there is a body of men upon earth for whom, more than for any other, I ought to cherish every feeling of attachment, superadded to every sentiment of reverence, it is the Senate of the United States. Its importance and dignity, as one of the branches of the legislature, as one of the component parts of the supreme executive, and as the tribunal of official honor and virtue, cannot be more highly estimated by any man than by me. My father had the honor of being its first presiding officer. I had, for five years, that of being one of its members; and through every successive administration of this Government, from the establishment of the national Constitution to this time, I have received frequent tokens of its confidence, which can never be obliterated from my memory, and claiming all my gratitude. For every individual member of the body I feel all the respect due to his public character; and there is not one member towards whom I entertain a sentiment other than that of regard and esteem. If, therefore, the principle upon which I have omitted to pay them first visits of form should ultimately fail of meeting their approbation, it will be serious cause of regret to me; but, at all events, I hope they will impute it to any other cause than intentional disrespect to them.

I take this occasion of observing that, with my approbation and advice, my wife has acted upon the same principle with regard to the ladies connected with members of the Senate or House of Representatives, who have visited this place during the sessions of Congress, that I have pursued in relation to the members themselves. She has paid no visits to ladies with whom she had not the advantage of being acquainted. She has received with pleasure and returned the visits of all ladies who have called upon her, whether connected with members of Congress or otherwise. She has visited her friends on the usual footing of private citizens, without pretension to claim, and without being sensible of any obligation to pay any first visit. She would have paid, with much pleasure, this compliment to the ladies of members of Congress, had it been proper, in her opinion, to confine it to them. But she was aware that many other ladies equally strangers to her, and, though not immediately allied to members of Congress, of character and standing in society equally respectable, occasionally came to spend some time in the city; and, knowing it to be impossible that she should visit them all, she declined the invidious task of discriminating whom she should and whom she should not first visit. If, in observing this rule, she has deviated from the practice of some other ladies in situations similar to her own, she has conformed to that which she constantly observed when she was herself the wife of a Senator at the seat of government. She then always called upon the ladies of the heads of departments when she came to Washington, and always understood it to be the common practice. She lays no claim, however, to the same attention from any other lady, and, having no pretension to visits of etiquette herself, thinks herself amenable to none from others. She has invited to her house, without waiting for formal visits, every lady of a member of Congress to whom she had not reason to believe such an invitation would be unwelcome; and, while feeling it as a favor from those who have accepted her invitations, she has only regretted the more rigorous etiquette of those who have declined, inasmuch as it bereft her of the happiness which she would have derived from a more successful cultivation of their acquaintance. She would regret still more the error which should, in any instance, attribute her conduct to a pretension of any kind on her part, or to a disregard of what is due from her to others.

I have thought this candid explanation of the motives of my conduct particularly due to those members of the Senate who, it has been intimated to me, have thought there was something exceptionable in it. I submit it to your indulgence and to their candor, with the sincere and earnest assurance of my perfect respect for yourself and them.

JOHN QUINCY ADAMS.

Appendix B.

Precedence of Diplomatic Agents in Force January, 1882.

*Regulations annexed to the Vienna Congress Treaty of June 9, 1815.**

IN order to prevent the inconveniences, which have frequently occurred and which might again arise, from claims of precedence among different Diplomatic Agents, the Plenipotentiaries of the powers who signed the Treaty of Paris, have agreed on the following articles, and they think it their duty to invite the Plenipotentiaries of the Crowned Heads to adopt the same regulations.

Article I.—Diplomatic Agents are divided into three classes : that of Ambassadors, Legates, or Nuncios : that of Envoy, Ministers, or other persons accredited to Sovereigns : that of Chargés d'Affaires accredited to Ministers for Foreign Affairs.

II.—Ambassadors, Legates or Nuncios only, have the Representative character.

* Burke's *Peerage,* page 1575.

III.—Diplomatic Agents on an extraordinary Mission have not, on that account, any superiority of rank.

IV.—Diplomatic Agents shall take precedence in their respective classes according to the date of the official notification of their arrival. The present Regulations shall not cause any innovation with regard to the Representative of the Pope.

V.—A uniform mode shall be determined in each scale for the Reception of Diplomatic Agents of each class.

VI.—Relations of Consanguinity, or of family alliance between Courts, confer no precedence on their Diplomatic Agents. The same rule also applies to political alliances.

VII.—In Acts or Treaties between several Powers which grant alternate precedence, the order which is to be observed in the signatures shall be determined by lot between the Ministers."

The present Regulation is inserted in the Protocol of the Plenipotentiaries of the eight Powers who signed the Treaty of Paris at their sitting of the 19th March, 1815.

Signed in the alphabetical order of the Courts by the principal Plenipotentiaries of Austria, (Espagne) Spain, France, Great Britain, Portugal, Prussia, Russia, Sweden.

PROTOCOL OF CONFERENCE OF THE FIVE POWERS. AIX-LA-CHAPELLE, NOVEMBER 21, 1818.

Ministers Resident.

In order to avoid inconvenient discussions which might in future arise upon a point of Diplomatic Etiquette, which appears not to have been anticipated in the Annex to the Treaty of Vienna, whereby questions of precedence were regulated, it is agreed between the five Courts, that Ministers Resident accredited to them, shall form with respect to their precedence, an intermediate class, between Ministers of the 2d class and Chargés d'Affaires.

Some Points of Etiquette.

INASMUCH as it is somewhat of a mooted point with regard to the social official precedence to which the Speaker may be entitled as the presiding officer of the House of Representatives, especially as relatively to the Chief Justice, who is the head of one of the three great Departments of the Government, it may not be uninstructive to give an opinion from a source of such recognized high authority as Mr. Robert C. Winthrop, of Boston. I desire, therefore, and it has been suggested, that it would be well, to publish some extracts from a letter I had the pleasure to receive from Mr. Winthrop, in which he says, " Your ' Etiquette' interested me not a little, and recalled some experiences of my own. On being elected Speaker in 1847, I consulted John Quincy Adams, then a member of the House, and the consequence was that I felt bound to call first only on the President and Vice-President. I believe I made an exception in favor of Chief-Justice Taney, but only as a matter of grace. There cannot be a doubt that the President, Vice-President, and Speaker stand before all others as the representatives of the

6   81

82   APPENDIX.

Executive and Legislative branches. I remember
how earnestly this was enforced upon us by Colonel
Benton, a great stickler for 'etiquette,' and who said
to me on one occasion, 'You may be as modest as
you please in regard to any matter personal to yourself, but you have no right to waive the priority of
your position and the dignity of the House of Representatives.' Everybody called on me first accordingly, except the President and Vice-President."

' In addition to this very decided opinion of Mr.
Winthrop, I am informed that the late Chief-Justice Chase also held that the Speaker should receive
the first visit, taking the ground that the Speaker,
being one of the possible contingent successors to the
Chief Magistracy, had a prior claim of social precedence over the Chief-Justice. How far the well-
known preference and proclivities of the late Chief-
Justice for political rather than judicial pre-eminence
may have shaped his judgment on this point is to be
considered.

I was taught to view the office of Chief-Justice
as the second place in the republic; indeed, my
dear father, the late Hon. S. F. Vinton, than whom
the country has never had a wiser statesman, held it
to be the first in true dignity, as raised far above the
strife and passions that must ever mark the political
career. Now, Mr. Vinton, having been a member of
the Lower House for nearly a quarter of a century,
during which he shaped some of its most important

legislation, must have been fully aware of all the possible claims attached to the position of Speaker. I know that he held this opinion in common with many other competent persons who are equally accomplished and instructed.

But, as I have already declared in this essay on "Etiquette," my sole object is to collate various expressions on these and other mooted points, in the hope that their presentation may lead to the establishment of more clearly defined rules. I am therefore equally pleased to publish opinions of weight when presented, whether they may happen to coincide with any preconceived notion of my own or not.

No one can overlook the almost supreme *political* significance to be attached to the office of Speaker, especially when this place is filled by an able statesman, as the incumbent is apt to be, nor the actual dignity of the position as apart from personal ability. The Speaker is the chosen head of that legislative branch which most truly and immediately represents the people,—not the irresponsible masses, but the organized people, which is sovereign.

In England the office of Speaker of the House of Commons is, as we all know, one of signal importance, and in point of social rank takes place next to the peers of Great Britain. A very large salary is attached to the office in order to enable the Speaker to hold Parliamentary levees and to give dinners to

the members of the House. However, no comparison,
it seems to me, can be properly instituted between
the office of the Speaker of the House of Commons
and that of the House of Representatives. The inherited successorship to the crown, I believe, gives
precedence in England above all other considerations, and perhaps, in viewing the positions of the
Vice-President and of the Cabinet, the contingent
Presidential successorship may be made to weigh in
the same sense. Yet it does not strike one as a very
republican view of the case, or one to which any
special weight ought to be attached in determining
the relative places of Vice-President, Speaker, and
Chief Justice. It would be more in accordance with
republican ideas to assign the *real* relative place according to their *real* functions, respectively as presiding officers of the various branches, legislative and
judicial.

Although the Chief Justice is appointed by the
President and confirmed by the Senate, yet *once created* he becomes the grand conservative element and
head of the nation, before whom the President himself may be arraigned in case of impeachment. He
moreover holds his exalted station for life, so that he
may do justice without fear or favor. He embodies,
in fact, the ultimate human conception and govern-
mental shadowing forth of godlike prerogatives, and
should receive the highest tokens of respect. We cannot too jealously guard intact such conservative force

as the Constitution gives us to be used as safeguards against the aggressive tendencies of a democracy.

There is also another matter upon which much confusion prevails, and that is with regard to first visits to be made between persons holding relatively the same office, as among Senators for instance. There exists a rough paper, endorsed in Mr. Jefferson's hand, concerning the etiquette of the Government, as agreed upon by General Washington, and it may serve a good purpose in this connection to transcribe it *entire.* It may assist to elucidate some other points equally unsettled at present. I have already republished the letter of John Quincy Adams, and when this paper of Mr. Jefferson is added I shall have given perhaps the only other published authority which may be brought to bear. Mr. Jefferson says :

" In order to bring the members of society together in the first instance, the custom of the country has established that residents shall pay the first visit to strangers, and, among strangers, first comers to later comers, foreign and domestic, the character of stranger ceasing after the first visit. To this rule there is a single exception. Foreign ministers, from the necessity of making themselves known, pay the first visit to the ministers of the nation, which is returned.

" I. When brought together in society, all are perfectly equal, whether foreign or domestic, titled or

untitled, in or out of office. All other observances
are but exemplifications of these two principles.

"First. The families of foreign ministers arriv-
ing at the seat of government receive the first visit
from those of the national ministers, as from all
other residents.

"Second. Members of the legislature and of the
judiciary, independent of their offices, have a right
as strangers to receive the first visit.

"II. First. No title being admitted here, those
of foreigners give no precedence.

"Second. Differences of grade among the diplomatic members give no precedence.

"Third. At public ceremonies, to which the Government invites the presence of foreign ministers and
their families, a convenient seat or station will be
provided for them, with any other strangers invited,
and the families of the national ministers, each taking
place as they arrive and without any precedence.

"Fourth. To maintain the principle of equality or
of *pêle-mêle*, and prevent the growth of precedence out
of courtesy, the members of the executive will prac-
tise at their own houses and recommend an adherence
to the ancient usage of the country, of gentlemen in
mass giving precedence to the ladies in mass in pass-

ing from one apartment where they are assembled to another." (Vol. ix., pp. 454–55, Jefferson's Works.)

Several points are to be noted in the perusal of this paper. Foreign ministers were "to pay the first visit to the ministers of the nation" simply "from the necessity of making themselves known" to the Government near which they are accredited; nor does this visit seem to have been exacted of them in other cases. Nor yet did this necessity *extend to their families*, but the reverse.

These rules, as given by Jefferson, enforce some official distinctions for the actual incumbent of office, and at the same time "perfectly equal" social status for all when brought together in society.

Of course, in a purely social point, one must expect and receive recognition as an "equal," or otherwise there can be, properly speaking, no social life. Yet there will arise public and other occasions of mere formal ceremony, in which the official position cannot be lost sight of, and at such times there should be no social misunderstanding.

There are *customs* which make a sort of supplementary law; as, for instance, in the case of addressing the President in writing. Here *polite usage* sanctions the address to "His Excellency," although the legislative enactment resolved that the address should be, "To the President of the United States," without addition of title.

Yet the very sentiment which caused so many divers committee reports before this resolution was reached, has notwithstanding, led to the adoption of some added title of respect among cultured people. In fact, a distinguished committee of conference, originally selected by both Houses to consider this matter, reported "that, in the opinion of the committee, it will be proper thus to address the President: 'His Highness, the president of the United States and Protector of their liberties.'" Undoubtedly the great personal veneration in which Washington was held swayed the republican minds of these legislators in this instance, although, fortunately for the permanence of our freedom, we escaped the infliction of the title of "Highness," as addressed to any American citizen.

www.ingramcontent.com/pod-product-compliance
Lightning Source LLC
Chambersburg PA
CBHW020809020726
47495CB00008B/2653